Pretty PRINCESSES

Beautiful Princesses to Color!

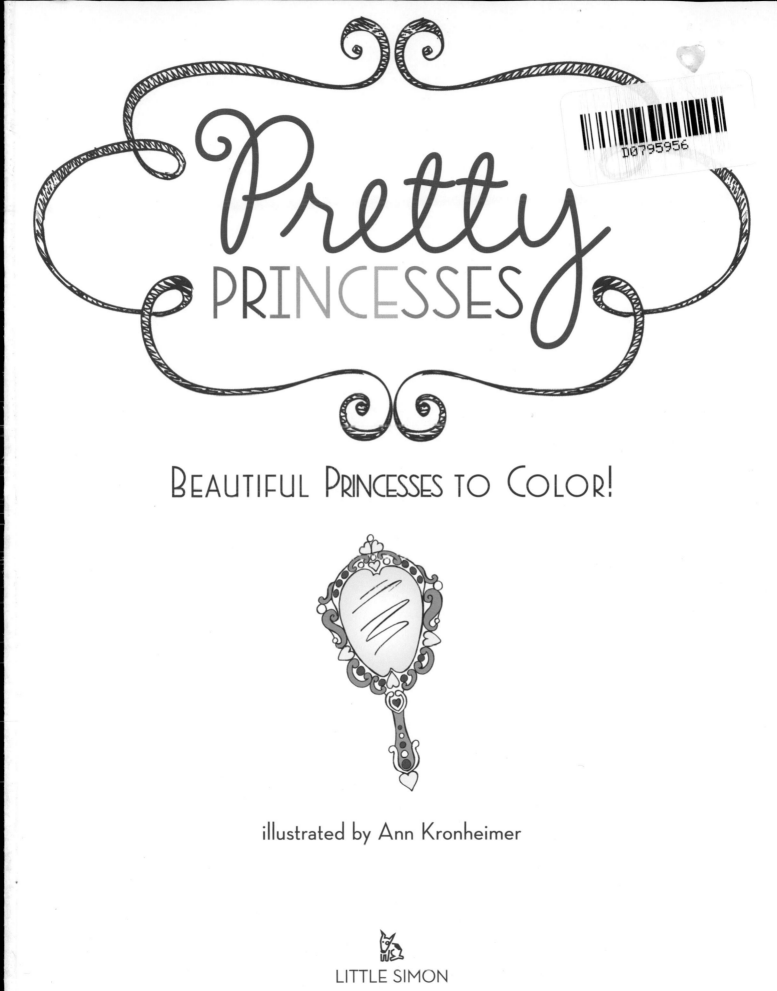

illustrated by Ann Kronheimer

LITTLE SIMON

New York London Toronto Sydney New Delhi

The illustrations in this book
were colored and completed by:

_____

LITTLE SIMON

An imprint of Simon & Schuster Children's Publishing Division

1230 Avenue of the Americas, New York, New York 10020

Copyright © 2014 by Buster Books, an imprint of Michael O'Mara Books, Ltd..

For information about special discounts for bulk purchases, please contact Simon & Schuster

Special Sales at 1-866-506-1949 or business@simonandschuster.com.

The Simon & Schuster Speakers Bureau can bring authors to your live event.

For more information or to book an event contact the Simon & Schuster Speakers Bureau at

1-866-248-3049 or visit our website at www.simonspeakers.com.

Manufactured in China 0214 SCP

10 9 8 7 6 5 4 3 2

ISBN 978-1-4424-8385-9

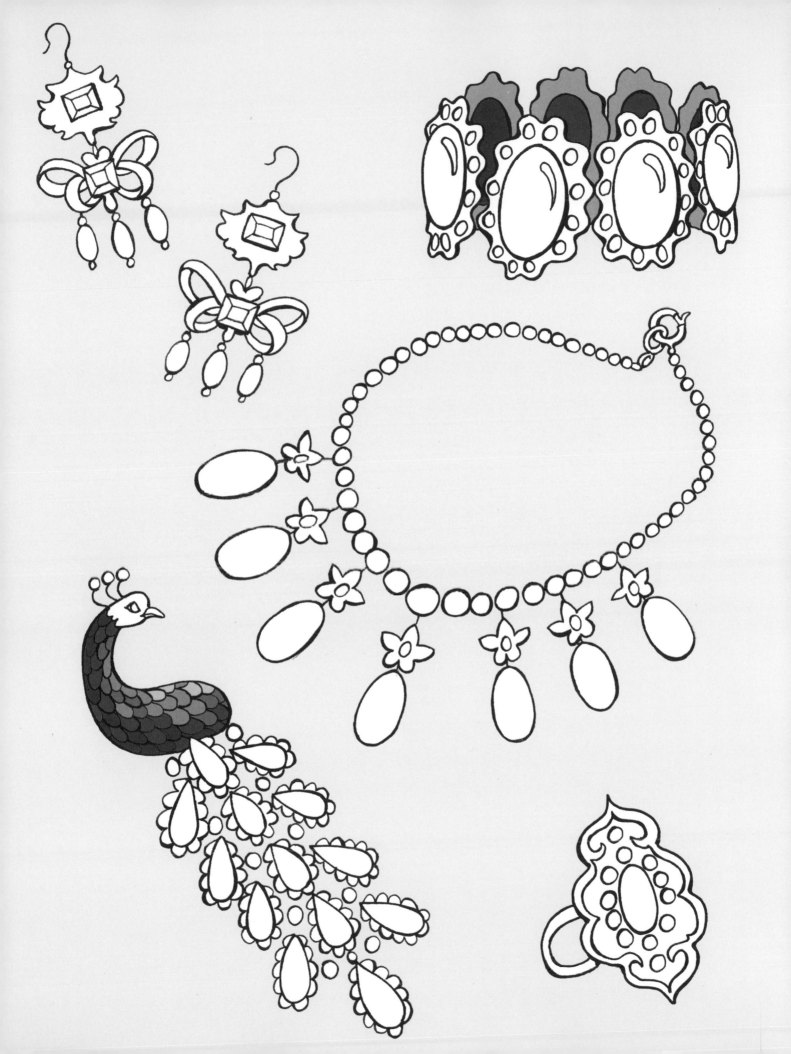